Little
Rabbit
waits for the
moon

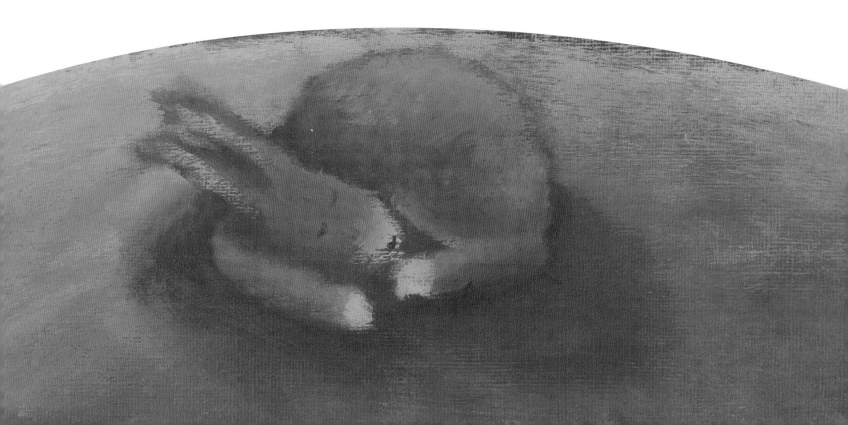

Text © Beth Shoshan 2004
Illustrations © Stephanie Peel 2004
This edition published by Parragon in 2010
Parragon, Queen Street House, 4 Queen Street, Bath BA1 1HE, UK
Published by arrangement with
Meadowside Children's Books , 185 Fleet Street,
London EC4A 2HS

A CIP catalogue record for this book is available
from the British Library
Printed in China

ISBN 978-1-4454-0796-8

Little Rabbit waits for the moon

Beth Shoshan and Stephanie Peel

Bath · New York · Singapore · Hong Kong · Cologne · Delhi · Melbourne

Little Rabbit
couldn't sleep...

In the day,
the sun is there, warm
and bright. But when night comes,
the sky hangs low, dark, and empty.

"If I fall asleep now, there'll be no one
watching over me," thought Little Rabbit.
"I'll just have to wait for the moon."
And so he did just that.

The trouble with being
so tired and sleepy,
was that he didn't
know exactly when
the moon would come.

Little Rabbit waited
and waited.

More time passed and the moon still hadn't come.

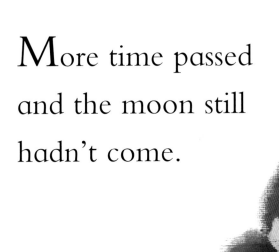

He thought he had better ask someone how much longer he might have to wait.

"This is my first day, ever,"
said a small flower in the fields.
"Maybe I will have grown into a tree
by the time your moon comes."

That sounded like a very long time.

Little Rabbit thought he had better ask
someone else—just to be sure.

"Look deep into the water," shimmered a little lake nearby. "Maybe your moon has fallen in and can't get out."

That didn't sound like what he wanted to hear.

Little Rabbit thought he had better ask someone else—just to be sure.

"Why don't you walk with me?"
twisted a long and winding path.
"We can find out where I'm leading
and maybe your moon is at the
other end!"

That sounded like it might
be a long way away.

Little Rabbit thought he had better ask
someone else—just to be sure.

"I've just blown in to these parts," breezed a wind that had picked up. "Who knows? I might be a big, fierce storm by the time your moon comes."

That didn't sound like something he wanted to wait for.

Little Rabbit thought he had better ask someone else—just to be sure.

"We can't see your moon yet,"
rumbled the great, rolling hills.
"And we can see far into
the distance from up here!"

That didn't sound very promising.

Little Rabbit began to think that the
moon might never come. And he was
getting very, very tired…

And then, from behind the hills,
carried by the wind along the twists
of the path, reflected in the lake, and shining
on the petals of the small flower...

...the most perfect moon
slid into the night sky.

But Little Rabbit
had fallen asleep, dreaming
of the moon that would
watch over him through the night.